*For Poppy, with love ~ M C B*

*For Toby ~ F E*

LITTLE TIGER PRESS LTD,
an imprint of the Little Tiger Group
1 Coda Studios, 189 Munster Road, London SW6 6AW
www.littletiger.co.uk

First published in Great Britain 2008
This edition published 2018

Printed in China • LTP/1400/2920/0819

10 9 8 7 6

# The Wishing Star

M Christina Butler

Frank Endersby

LITTLE TIGER
LONDON

Little Brown Mouse and
Little Grey Mouse were the
very best of friends. They
did everything together.
    "I'm so glad you
come with me on my
adventures," said
Little Brown Mouse.
"It wouldn't be much
fun by myself."

"I am so lucky to have
you as a friend," said
Little Grey Mouse.
"I wouldn't dare climb
so high without you!"

They went everywhere
together and always
looked after each
other.

They shared everything, even
their biggest secrets and
special dreams.

One night, as the two friends sat
planning their next adventure, they
saw a glittering star shoot across
the sky and fall into the lake.

"It's a Wishing Star!" cried Little Brown Mouse. "We can make a wish, if we find it!"

He raced down the hill. "Come on!" he shouted. "We'll go in our boat down the river!"

"All the way to the lake?" Little Grey Mouse squeaked, running after him. "That's dangerous!"

But by the time he caught up, Little Brown Mouse was pushing their boat into the water.

"We must hurry!" he said. "We must find the star before anyone else does!"

As they floated down the river, strange shadows
moved through the reeds in the moonlight.

"Are you sure we're safe?" Little Grey Mouse
asked nervously.

Little Brown Mouse didn't answer. He was
paddling with all his might and thinking about
what he would wish for when they found the star.

"I shall wish to have an exciting adventure every day!" he said, paddling harder than ever.

"And I shall wish for a magic larder that is always full of nuts and berries," began Little Grey Mouse dreamily.

"No! No!" shouted Little Brown
Mouse, leaping up. "We can only
have one wish, because there is
only one star!"

"But we need food for
the winter!" cried Little
Grey Mouse, stamping
his foot.

"I saw the star first!"
Little Brown Mouse
replied crossly.
"The wish belongs
to me!"

And as the two mice argued,
the boat rocked and
twisted round
and round,
until . . .

all at once, it bumped into the
reeds and stopped. The mice
peered out into the darkness.
"Is this where the water
monsters live?" whispered
Little Grey Mouse, trembling.

He grabbed on to Little Brown Mouse.
There was something rustling in the reeds!
"Eeeek!" he squeaked with a jump, as two
bright eyes stared out at them.
"What are you two doing here?"
cried Vole in surprise.

Little Brown
Mouse sighed with relief.

"Please help us, Vole. We're
on our way to find a Wishing Star
that's fallen in the lake, but now
we're stuck!"

"A Wishing Star?" Vole shivered
with excitement. "I shall wish for
a fresh bed of grass every day,
then I won't have to make my bed
any more!"

"Did you say a Wishing Star in the lake?" croaked Frog, hopping up out of the river. "I shall wish for as many flies as I can eat!" And with a huge leap he was gone!

"Quick! We must go!" cried Vole, jumping into the water and giving the mice new paddles. "We can't let Frog get there before us!"

Vole pushed the leaf boat from the reeds, then scrambled aboard as the wind took hold of it and sent them speeding down the river.

Twirling and swirling, the boat
was swept this way and that
between the rocks. Little Grey
Mouse held on tightly and thought
about his warm, cosy bed under
the oak tree, when suddenly he
heard a loud CROAK!

"Look over there!" he cried out. "Frog's trapped
on the rocks! We must help him!"

"I suppose so," muttered Little Brown Mouse,
guiding the boat across to Frog. "Even though he
was going to take our wish for himself!"

"Thank you," Frog
spluttered as Little
Grey Mouse
pulled him
to safety.

They huddled together as the boat
swirled on, until at last the water grew
calmer and slower as they came nearer
to the lake.

"One more bend," said Vole eagerly,
"and we shall be there!"

Gently they drifted on to the lake, and there before
them were hundreds of shimmering Wishing Stars!
    "*Look!*" gasped Little Grey Mouse. "We can *all*
have a wish!"
    "And you must go first," said Little Brown Mouse.
    Little Grey Mouse smiled and thought hard.
"I wish," he said slowly, "I wish, that I shall always
have such good friends as you!"
    And they all agreed, that was the best wish ever!